Butterflying:

The Musicals

The Long and

the Short of it.

Synopsis, Plot

and

Words to

Songs

Also includes the text of a first short musical:

A LITTLE BUTTERFLY(ING)

Copyrights

Contents

SYNOPSIS

BUTTERFLYING - THE MUSICAL COMPLETE VERSION IN FIVE ACTS

ACT 1 Scene I

Heidelberg, Summer 2000

D. meets E. when on a summer language course in Heidelberg. D. is keen on music, dancing and shows and someone suggests that he goes and meets E. thinking that that would get on well together, since she loves dancing. A man tells D. that E. teaches German to children and D. waits outside of the classroom for a while. He knocks. She comes to the door. She is Polish with green feline eyes and very beautiful. They introduce each other by name and the first thing she does is to dance the Argentinian tango with him in the corridor. He immediately falls in love with her and loses his heart in Heidelberg to her. They star in a student show together and perform a routine to 'Ich hab' mein Herz in Heidelberg verloren'. (Other covers could be from The Student Prince.' He changes into a tuxedo and sings Recondita Armonia and O Sole Mio *may need permission(for these songs but they could be swapped for other songs. It would be a happy ending but after the show when D. wants to go back home and hopefully take her with him, E. stands chatting to other hunky male students. He visits her often in her student flat. Sometimes she goes out with other people e.g. for the whole evening and to a show *leaving him alone in the flat to his own devices, mainly cleaning, cooking and getting surprises ready for her). And he is so in love that he just accepts her behaviour and waits for her to return. He cooks, cleans , washes dishes and buys her presents. She returns and he is so happy to see her. After the language course is over, he returns to Cambridge for his second year studying German and Spanish, heartbroken at leaving her behind in Heidelberg.

Scene II

2000-2001 – Cambridge University

Exchange of love letters. D. is more in love with E. than E. is with D. Examples of D. missing E. in songs and he reads out his love letters.

ACT II –Scene 1

Munich Granada 2001-2002

D. is studying at LMU Munich for his year abroad. He meets U. in a local choir St Josefskirche and she is quite attractive and very natural but a bit childish. They soon become good friends and go on a few dates, meeting each other in Munich, walking around Munich and she introduces D. to her male friends, A. (who has had a nervous breakdown of sorts or is low on confidence) and M. (who works for BMW but cannot find a girlfriends at the moment and has been 'friends# with U. for years. However, U. is very immature and naïve. When he learns that he even has to teach her how to kiss, D. becomes suspicious and thinks she might be a virgin. Nothing happens between them more than a few kisses goodnight and D. is wondering what he going on. Also he cannto seem to forget his Polish butterfly, E., and he keeps thinking of her. Following a group holiday in Greece with U. A. and M. in a hired car going around the Peloponese, U. loses her wallet and accuses D. of stealing it, whereupon he falls out with her temporarily. The wallet soon turns up at the lost and found, but in the interim U. asks. D. to pay for everything and like a fool, he obliges, feeling sorry for her. When the wallet turns up, U. forgets to reimburse D. thinking it traditional that the man should pay for everything. Also, later on the holiday, other ridiculous and hilarious incidents take place, especially on the beach with her beach attire, revealing a stupid side to U. D. had not noticed in Munich. After the holiday, D. returns to his shared student flat in Schwabing in Munich. He manages to move to a different flat in the same complex which he has been waiting fro since day one, since he has been put in the loudest room on Campus, above the student bar and they play music all night on Monday nights every week and other surprise days of the week until the early hours and this ruins hiss sleep and so he cannot concentrate in his lectures and seminars. After moving from Albrechtstrasse to Adelheidstrasse he takes the opportunity to make a clean break with U. and does not tell him that he has moved.

Act III

D. sends E. an email. She is still in Heidelberg. She emails him back that she wants to go on a language course in Granada and since he is learning Spanish as well, he wants to go as well. He phones her from his newly acquired mobile phone. They go to Granada. D. blows it, since he has to much to drink and this leads to him start smoking again and for the whole night one cigarette after the next and so he comes back to the flat stinking of cigarettes and alcohol and she naturally hates that of course. D. is so happy to be in Granada and drinks too much wine, triggering his addiction to smoking again. At any rate, that night, he is told in no uncertain terms to sleep on a couch next door and not together as they were at the start of the trip. Over the next few days D. can sense that he is losing her. She gets up early and visits the Alhambra, where you have to queue up dead early and since he is hungover and she fails to wake him, he misses seeing the Alhambra. He pretends he does not mind and decides to take Flamenco guitar lessons while she goes to Spanish language lessons and also with the motive of impressing E. He buys a flamenco guitar to impress her and boots. J. (male) is a good teacher and teaches D. all about Flamenco and the passion of the guitar. The lessons are all in Spanish, so D. convinces himself that he is learning Spanish at the same time, rather than going to the language school in Granada. The trip to Granada comes to a natural end and they catch the bus back to Malaga, but she is tired of D. by now and before they reach the hotel to stay overnight before flying back, she suggests that they go their separate ways . But he waits for her outside a bar, where she is chatting to a Spanish guy, practising her newly acquired Spanish from the language course. Despite being jealous, he fells he can trust her, because he is in love with her and he knows she is a little naïve too and a bit of a show-off like himself. So he waits for her, patiently for hours until she finished her evening and he is outside the bar in the street and on a bench etc. They fly back to Frankfurt am Main and then there is some confusion over the train that they are going to catch next. D. is supposed to be returning to Munich. E. wants to go to Heidelberg and asks D. to go with her. A man in the train suggests to D. that this girl really likes D. and D. would be a complete and utter idiot not to accompany her to Heidelberg. Then they go back to her student flat and spend a few happy days as friends but still D. would like to have more romance, kisses, cuddles and a more physical relationship. Then one day, D. tells D. she is going back home to se her mother in Poland. She lives in Sanok, on the Russian border. D. agrees to help her with her luggage and they get the train together from Heidelberg to Frankfurt am Main again. Once again, in the confusion that ensues at the railway station, D. fails to return to Munich, helping E. all the time with her things and what she has to do to book in and everything for the flight to Poland. She then suggests he might come with her and he jumps at the chance, but the flight costs a small fortune, because he has not booked in advance and it was not planned at all. They fly to Krakow.

Act IV – Scene I Krakow Sanok Munich 2001-2002

Krakow Sanok

On the plane to Krakow, she drops the bombshell that it would be better if he stayed at the University in Krakow in a student room. He gets a room there and does a little sightseeing while she books a train ticket to Sanok and goes home to see her mother. D. feels neglected and alone in Krakow. After a day or so, E. calls and suggests that he travels on the train to Sanok and so he goes there alone and meets her at Sanok station. She takes him to a tiny flat where her mother lives, Her father dies years ago. She has a sister, too, but she is no longer living there. After not being overtly sexual at all, only a few kisses, in a room right next to her mother, where everything would be audible, E. makes a complete pass at D. D. is mortified because he wants her so much , but is totally frustrated since he wanted a romantic location to make love to her. And so he is unable to respond to her wishes, although he absolutely would love to have sex with her, this is just the wrong location. Out of respect for her mother, with whom he seems to get along with quite well, despite the language barrier, D. withdraws from the clinch. He is shocked by E.'s advances since this is the first time she has acted like this. (With hindsight, D. feels he has blown it again, completely by repelling her advances and not just going along with it all. They visit the local church and D. imagines that they will get married there.

Scene IV - E. visits him again in Munich and it is a strange night. D. had booked tickets to an opera, Madame Butterfly and his friend from Cambridge who lives in Munich, A., is waiting with D. at his flat to meet E. as well. E. is late and A. keeps saying to D. that E. has let him down and is clearly not coming. Maybe he should have the ticket to the opera and come with D. D. feels something is not right and just is sure that E. would be turning up in Munich and coming to his flat. He goes alone to Munich train station. There he finds E. wandering around the platforms looking like a lost little girl. They rush to the opera and are late for it and have lost their special seats that he reserved specially and at considerable cost and they have to sit in worse seats. D. returns back to his flat, she goes back to Heidelberg the next day. He then goes back to Cambridge the following week with a flamenco guitar, another acoustic guitar he has bought in Munich and tons of luggage.

Act V - Cambridge University

Scene I

D. invites L. (a Romanian student he has met in Munich) to visit him in Cambridge and has been emailing E. as well. They both decide to come the same weekend. L. arrives first with a boyfriend in tow, called, W. Much comedy ensues, the room is not good enough for her boyfriend and he threatens to leave. He does not think D. can understand his German but D. can. He has reserved a really good room for L. and it is a little small, because he did not know two people were arriving. He is a bombastic, tight-fisted, domineering, controlling man, who pays for nothing and expects D. to pay for all their trips in and around Cambridge, to the Ely Cathedral and he won't even buy L. fish and chips, so D. in the end pays for sandwiches for both of them. He is an organist in a church on the outskirts of Munich and a good twenty years older than L. L. and W. are in D.'s student room in the main College where he is a student and are waiting for E. to arrive. D. has had an email that she is coming and flying from Frankfurt. He assumes it to be Frankfurt am Main and works out when she will arrive. D. goes to Cambridge train station with L. and W. to meet her and later even Stanstead airport on his own, but she is not there and D. returns empty-handed to his room in College. She does not show up and L. and W, just like A. in the previous Act, tell D. that E. is not the right lady for him to marry. They go to bed in Bennet House, E. still not having shown up. D. goes to bed alone too. E. has told D. that she is flying in from Frankfurt to Stanstead. In the early hours of the morning D. has a dream that E. is outside and he can swear he hears her voice, calling D. D. D. D. In fact, it is E. outside his window, shouting up at him. He goes down to collect her. She has flown from Frankfurt an der Oder, which is cheaper with Ryan Air and has been waiting in fields and waiting rooms for hours and hence the delay in showing up. D. is so happy to see her, since he loves her and forgives her and trusts her once again. The four friends spend time together in Cambridge. But E. wants to go to Kings College for evensong and there is only 1 ticket for this college available. They have four available for St John's evensong. E. takes the sole ticket for Kings and goes alone which makes the other three who go to St Johns further doubt E.'s intentions of having a relationship with D. L. and W. continue to advise D. and warn him off. They drift apart.

Scene II – Oxford University 2004

D. breaks a joint in his back moving rooms, He is doing a Masters at Oxford, after leaving Cambridge University. At Oxford, he has received a love letter from E. He goes into the lecture theatre where there is a grand piano and practises before and after lectures for hours, composing his romantic piano music and love songs. HE sings some of them.

Scene III - Frankfurt – Heidelberg – 2006

Whilst visiting his brother in Frankfurt in 2006 with his mum and dad, D. decides to go off and visit E. in Heidelberg for one day. She has moved rooms to the other side of the Neckar. She tells him that, in the interim period, she met a man called D. (same name as D.) from Cambridge who was an internationally renowned orchestra leader. They got engaged. She became pregnant. It turns out that this other D. mistreated her and she had to have an abortion. This is all rather a lot for D. to swallow. He is heartbroken that she went with this other man. D. is presently doing a Phd by living at home with his parents and commuting to a University in London to see his supervisor. He moots the idea of the leitmotif of the butterfly in German literature with his supervisor, who does not understand him. He has met his supervisor at Oxford but he teaches at London University as well, so D. can meet him in Oxford and in London. As Oxford is close they meet, first in coffee bars and then in Christchurch College Oxford. They had conversations about E. and butterflies, but Professor V. suggests he takes on the subject of metamorphosis rather than butterflies. D. still misses E. and writes lots of music about her.

TEXT OF FIRST SHORT MUSICAL: A LITTLE BUTTERFLY(ING)

BUTTERFLYING THE SHORT MUSICAL

SET at ST. EDMUND'S COLLEGE CAMBRIDGE

TIME PERIOD: 1999-2003

THREE AREAS ON THE STAGE
LIGHTING SHIFTS DEPENDING ON THE SCENE

AREA A: JUNIOR COMMON ROOM AREA - A sofa at the back of the stage with a table and newspapers. Tea and Coffee on a trolley. Biscuits.

AREA B: DINING ROOM CORNER WITH PIANO, ONE DINING ROOM TABLE WITH CHAIRS.

AREA C: CHAPEL AREA – AREA WHERE ALL THE DANCING, and CONCERTS TAKE PLACE AND THE MASS FOR THE WEDDING

CAST:

MAIN CHARACTERS : D. E. A. M. T. L. W.
OTHER STUDENTS (CHORUS)
LECTURERS/ COLLEGE OFFICERS

CLOTHING: DRESSED LIKE STUDENTS, HOODIES , JEANS, ROWING SWEATSHIRTS, RUGBY OR FOOTBALL.

BACKGROUND OF COLLEGE
Basically this was a really poor College in Cambridge, an old hall founded by monks and had only just recently got University status. The old Roman Catholic College in Cambridge. Other students had never ever heard of it and when the name is ever mentioned "St Edmund's", everyone always expresses surprise that it is a real College or they ask where it is, because they have never heard of it, because it is not like the other Church of England established Colleges like Trinity, King's, St John's, Emmanuel, which have had hundreds of years of tradition. St Edmund's is primarily for mature research students, mostly international ones, who speak poor English and are usually in about their 6th year of "pretending" to do a Phd. Also there are elite rowers, rugby and football players and ringers from America who are sporty, and athletic. There are a handful of Undergraduates, of which D. is one. He is studying languages, but all his fellow students are baffled by this, saying he is wasting his time and should study Law, Medicine or the Natural Sciences like themselves to earn loads of money in a later career. They are mainly Chinese, Japanese, Indian, German, French, from the USA or Australia or New Zealand, all studying law or medicine, mainly. He first meets A. from Munich, who is studying Physics but is a gifted singer and he sings Tenor and leads the Choir. He has also met a Japanese male student called M., who is studying History. M. can play the guitar, particularly *Los recuerdos de la Alhambra* by Barrios and a Finnish student called T. who is a Musicology student and plays the piano accompanying D. when he sings songs in the dining room and then when they have concerts in the Chapel.

ABRIDGED PLOT

D. is a student and spends his time sitting in the JCR pretending to read newspapers with an Emeritus Fellow, Professor of History. D. and Professor Jackman sitting on a sofa. D. is studying Modern Languages, but spends all his time in the dining room, trying to compose music on the upright piano, which is there by the door on the left. He is in love with E. a Polish butterfly, whom he met on a summer language course in Heidelberg. He misses her terribly because she is in Heidelberg and he has lost his heart there on the Summer Course in 2000. She loves acting, drama, dancing and especially the Argentinian tango. D. is captivated by her and compares her to a butterfly, fluttering around all the time. E. is still over there living in a student flat with girls and he is here, dreaming about her and talking to his Japanese friend, M. about her. It is a mixed

College so there are also many women. One weekend in his final year, D. invites E. and L. to come and visit him.

RED BOOK

ColdOutside(YourLove)

It's cold outside
It's cold outside your love

Your Love has gone Now it's time to carry on With my life

Oh come back Baby come back Into my arms

Oh come back Oh come back Come back for ever
Come back forever Forever

Now you can carry on with your life
Now you can concentrate your mind and soul And it's alright
The sun will shine In your eyes again

FEMALE VOICES
SOLO VERSES
CHORUS

Chardonnay

1.

Did you walk away again?
You couldn't ask for more my friend
You were living on Paradise Street
With the best girl you could ever hope to meet
But you blew (threw) it all away
When the girls came out to play
With a stream of cigarettes Beer, Schnaps and Chardonnay

FEMALE VOICE

2.

Did you walk away again? (Addressed to E.)
You were living at Rainbow's End
You were living on Paradise Street
With the best guy you could ever hope to meet
But you threw it all away
When the guys came out to play
With a stream of cigarettes
Red wine and Chardonnay

MALE VOICE

It never happened (So you told yourself) As you hid all the junk

FEMALE CHORUS

It never happened (So you told yourself) But you were out to lunch

FEMALE CHORUS

You pour it in a glass, but the bottle's gone anyway

FEMALE CHORUS

Along with your friends you knew from yesterday

FEMALE CHORUS

(Just like your friends you knew from yesterday)

D.sings...
But my heart's on fire, I'm on fire now
A will to power, nothing can stop me now
Mr. Mojo Risin's gone but Aida Dahlvrlegg's here anyhow
Just one Schnaps and tequila
Nothing can stop me now
They took my dreams away
But they're coming back today

Mariposa (sung by D.

Con esa canción
Con esa música

Quiero decirte
Quiero recordarte
Quiero expresarte
Quiero no olvidarte

Yo no te olvidaré
Nunca jamás
Yo no te olvidaré
Nunca jamás

Yo no te olvidaré, la razón es por que
Yo no te olvidaré, la razón es por que
Te adoro, no puedo olvidarte
Te adoro, no puedo olvidarte

Aunque te vayas, no sé a dónde Aunque te vayas, no sé a dónde Aunque vayas, no sé a dónde vayas Aunque vueles, no sé a dónde vueles

Mi mariposa
¿Cuando llegarás? Dulcinea
¿Cuando llegarás? Mariposa, tu vida es fugaz

¿A mi lado, cuando estarás?
¿En mi jardín, cuando estarás?

Schmetterling

Mit diesem Song
Mit diesem kleinen Liedchen
Möchte ich ja sagen
Möchte ich Dich erinnern
Möchte ich ja nur äußern
Möchte ich Dir sagen

Ich vergesse Dich nicht
Niemals
Ich vergesse Dich nicht
Niemals

Ich vergesse Dich nicht,
der Grund dafür ist
Über alles liebe ich Dich
Auf ewig liebe ich Dich
Ich kann Dich nicht vergessen

Obwohl Du weggehst,
wohin weiß ich nicht
Obwohl Du weggehst,
wohin weiß ich nicht
Obwohl Du wegfliegst,
wohin weiß ich nicht
 Obwohl Du wegfliegst,
wohin weiß ich nicht

An meiner Seite,
wann wirst Du da sein?

In meinem Garten, wann wirst Du da sein?
Meine Süsse, wann bist Du denn hier?
Mein Schmetterling, Dein Leben ist flüchtig

Butterfly

With this song
I just wanna say
With this little song
I just wanna say

With this little song
I just want to say
With this little piece of night music
I just want to say

I want to say to you
I want to remind you in my own way
I want to express myself today
I don't want to forget you

I'll never forget you
Never never forget you
Never never forget you
Never never forget you
Can't ever forget you
Can't ever forget you

Although you go away
Don't know which way
Although you go away
Don't know which way

Although you fly away where I do not know ...
Although you fly away where I do not know...

When will you be here at my side?
In my garden, when will you be there?
My butterfly, when will you arrive?
Oh sweetest one, when will you be there?
My butterfly, your life is fleeting...

Papillon

Par cette chanson Je voulais juste dire

Avec cette petite chanson Je voulais dire

Avec cette petite chanson Je voulais juste dire

Avec cette petite musique de nuit Je voulais juste dire

Je voulais te dire

Que je veux te rappeler, à ma façon Je veux m'exprimer à présent

Je ne veux pas t'oublier
Je ne t'oublierai jamais jamais. Jamais t'oublier. Jamais t'oublier
Jamais t'oublier Jamais t'oublier

Je ne pourrai jamais t'oublier
Je ne pourrai jamais t'oublier

Même si tu pars loin Je ne sais où

Même si tu pars loin
Ne sachant pas par quel chemin

Même si tu voles loin, je ne sais où
Même si tu voles loin je ne sais où

Quand seras-tu ici à mes côtés?
Dans mon jardin, quand seras-tu là?

Mon papillon, quand arriveras-tu?

Oh, ma plus douce, quand seras-tu là?
Mon papillon, ta vie est éphémère...

Edytka Butterfly

Edytka
Aida butterfly
Soar higher and higher and higher
Into the blue sky

Edytka
Aida butterfly
Soar higher and higher and higher
Into the night sky

My angel in flight
You fly out of my sight
Edytka
Aida butterfly
Higher and higher and higher
Into the night sky

Verse 1:

I wish I could fly
So high, high in the sky
Why do you flutterby?
Stay awhile my butterfly

Chorus 1:

Butterfly, there is something you can do
Show me how to fly around like you

Verse 2:

So sing, sing like a lark
Green cat's eyes that glow in the dark
And dance, you dance with such ease
Floating around into the breeze

Chorus 2:
Butterfly, there is something you can do
Teach me how to be just like you

Verse 3:
In my arms for a minute or two
That is all I ask of you
And a kiss savoured like red wine
From a goddess approaching the divine

Chorus 3:

Butterfly, there is something you can do
Reserve for me a tango dance or two (echo: with you, for two)

Verse 4:
I wish I could fly
Soar higher and higher and higher
Into the night sky
Don't fly away, apple of my eye
Be forever my butterfly

Chorus 4:
Oh Butterfly, show me the way

The truth and the light
Won't you forever stay?

Verse 5:

In my arms, forever mine
In your arms, forever thine
In our arms, forever entwined
In our arms, forever entwined

BLUE BOOK

These songs should be played in the key of moderation, moderately fast, moderately slow, medium paced not for too long just a moderate length of time.

Butterfly 2

With this song
With this music
With this little night music

I just want to say
I just want to remind you
I want to express

I just want to say
Remind you in my own way
Express myself today

I'll never forget you Never never
Never forget you Never never

Can't ever forget you
Though I close my eyes
Can't ever forget you
Why is that a surprise surprise?

Although you go away
Don't know which way
Although you go away
Don't know which way

Although you fly away
Where I do not know
Although you fly away
Where I do not know

My butterfly, when will you arrive?
Sweetest one, when will you be there?
Butterfly, try not to forget
Your life is fleeting ...
Don't say it's over yet
Don't say it's over yet

Butterfly 3

1.

I wish I could fly
So high in the sky

Why do you flutter by?
Stay awhile my Butterfly

2.

So sing, sing like a lark
Cat's eyes, that glow (shine) in the dark

And dance, you dance with such ease
Floating away into the breeze
Butterfly there's something you can do
Teach me how to fly away with you

Stay awhile this time it will be true
Show me how to fly around like you
Butterfly there's something you can do
Teach me how to fly away with you

Stay awhile this time it will be true
Show me how to fly around like you
Butterfly there's something you can do
Teach me how to fly away with you

Stay awhile this time it will be true
Show me how to fly around like you

Butterfly there's something you can do

Teach me how to fly away with you
Stay awhile this time it will be true
Show me how to fly around like you

Chardonnay 2

Did I walk away again?
I couldn't ask for more my friend I was living on Paradise Street
With the best girl I could ever hope to meet

But I blew (threw) it all away
When the dolls came out to play
With a stream of cigarettes Beer, Schnaps and Chardonnay
Red wine, Port and Chardonnay

Why did you walk away my friend? (Addressed to E.)
You were living at Rainbow's End
You were living on Paradise Street
With the best guy you could ever hope to meet

But you threw it all away
I pushed too soon that day
When the guys came out to play
With your Menthol cigarettes, lip-gloss and Chardonnay

It never happened you tell yourself
Hiding all the proof
When I asked you to marry me
What did you say?
It never happened I told myself
As I hid all my cigarettes
It never happened, so I told myself
But I was out to lunch

I poured it in a glass, but the bottle was gone anyway
Just like my friends I knew from yesterday

My heart's on fire I am on fire now
Mojo Risin's gone
Regallag Divad's here anyhow...

ColdOutside(yourLove)Silver and Gold Version

It's cold outside, cold outside your love
Your Love has gone
Now it's time to carry on
With my life

Oh come back... baby come back...
Into my arms
Oh come back... Oh come back...
Come back for ever
Come back forever
Forever

Now you can carry on with your life
Now you can concentrate your mind and soul
And it's alright
The sun will shine
In your eyes again

La Farfalla

Con questa musica, con questa canzone
Vorrei solo dire, vorrei ricordati

Non ti dimenticheró, proprio mai
Non ti dimenticheró, no no mai

Sebbene tu vada, vada via
Anche se tu vada via

Non so dove tu voli
Non so dove tu voli

In che direzione tu vada via
Ovunque vai, tu vada via

La farfalla, quando sarai qui
Dulcinea, quando sarai qui

La farfalla, la vita è bella[5]
 La farfalla, quando sarai qui

Mariposa 2

Con esa canción
Con esa música
Quiero decirte
Quiero recordarte
Quiero expresarte
Quiero no olvidarte

Yo no te olvidaré
Nunca jamás
Yo no te olvidaré
Nunca jamás

Yo no te olvidaré
La razón es por que
Yo no te olvidaré
La razón es por que
Te adoro
Te adoro

Aunque te vayas, no sé a dónde
Aunque te vayas, no sé a dónde
Aunque te vayas, no sé
A dónde vayas, no sé
Aunque vueles, no sé

Mi mariposa, ¿cuando llegarás?
Dulcinea, ¿cuando llegarás?
Mariposa, tu vida es fugaz

¿A mi lado, cuando estarás?
¿En mi jardín, cuando estarás?

Quizás (Spanish Translation of Maybe)

Quizás esta vez, verás, yo no soy el culpable
Quizás volverás a mí,
Quizás será el mismo de nuevo
Quizás

Hubieras pensado por ahora lo hubiera aprendido mi lección
Hubieras pensado esta vez que supiera mejor
Aquí voy otra vez, enamorándome de ti

Quizás esta vez, verás, yo no soy el culpable
Quizás volverás a mí,
Quizás será el mismo de nuevo

Quizás

Hubieras pensado por ahora lo hubiera aprendido mi lección
Hubieras pensado esta vez que supiera mejor
Aquí voy otra vez, enamorándome de ti

TheSameOldSlowDance

Verse 1:

Kiss me in the morning
And love me at night
I'll always watch out for you
Make sure I hold you tight

Chorus:

Because you're everything
And I've waited for all time
To make you mine

Verse 2:

Be my friend forever
Let me be the one
Who picks you up when you fall down
I'll always be around

Chorus:

Because you're everything
And I've waited for all time
To make you mine

You are the first face I want to see in the morning
You are the last face I want to look at... at night
You are the only face I want to see when it's over

The last eyes at the end of my world

Ooh... I love you... forever ... I love you
Forever... forever....forever... I love you
Forever

Schmetterling (1)

Mit diesem Liedchen
Mit diesem kleinen Liedchen
Mit dieser Musik
Mit dieser kleiner Nachtmusik

Möchte ich ja sagen
Möchte ich dich erinnern
Möchte ich mich ausdrücken

Ich vergesse Sie nicht (Dich)
Niemals

Ich vergesse dich nicht
Der Grund dafür ist
Über alles liebe ich dich
Im tiefsten Inneren liebe ich dich

(Ich) kann dich nicht vergessen (Ich) kann dich nicht vergessen

Obwohl du weggehst, wohin weiß ich nicht
Obwohl du weggehst, wohin weiß ich nicht
Obwohl du fliegst, weiß ich nicht
Obwohl du fliegst, weiß ich nicht

Mein Schmetterling, wann wirst du da sein?
Meine Süsse, wann bist du denn hier/da?
An meiner Seite, wann kommst du endlich?
In meinem Garten, wann wirst Du da sein?

Schmetterling (Ich vergesse dich nie)

Mit diesem Song
Mit diesem kleinen Song (chen)

Möchte ich nur sagen
Möchte ich dir sagen
Möchte ich dich erinnern
Möchte ich dir sagen

Ich vergesse dich nicht
Niemals, nie

Ich vergesse dich nicht
Der Grund dafür ist
Über alles, liebe ich dich
Auf ewig liebe ich dich

Kann dich nicht vergessen

Obwohl du weggehst, wohin weiß ich nicht
Obwohl du weggehst, wohin weiß ich nicht
Obwohl du wegfliegst, wohin weiß ich nicht
Obwohl du wegfliegst, wohin weiß ich nicht

An meiner Seite, wann wirst Du da sein?
In meinem Garten, wann wirst Du da sein?
Meine Süsse, wann bist du denn hier?
Mein Schmetterling, das Leben ist kurz
Mein Schmetterling, das Leben ist so kurz

t alone again

The Wind

1.

Anyway the wind blows Just like the grass grows Where does the wind go?
No one knows
No one knows

2.

Why does the sun set?
When will it be time?
How does the sun shine?
No one knows

Chorus 1:

A gust comes up
Whistling through the trees
A dark stranger appears In the Breeze

3.

Just as the bough breaks Just as the day breaks
What makes the wind blow?
No one knows

Chorus 2:

It drives the waves
Crashes and roars
The stranger appears
Once more (on the shore)

Chords:

The songs all have music composed for them which I know by heart and in some cases as I am so sure of the music I simply have not always written down all the chords in the songbook. Many recordings exist that I have copywritten and I hope soon to be able to produce music on manuscript paper in a forthcoming volume. All recordings and manuscript copies were copywritten and sent to my home address long ago by postal copyrighting methods. I am, however, providing some guitar chords for the following songs which is deliberately and totally confusing since all of them are played on a piano in the musical.

RED BOOK

Cold Outside (Your Love)

Verse: G D# G D# A# G# A# G# Gm Chorus: Am A# F E Bm F#m G Em Bm A Em A Em G Bm G Bm Emaj

Mariposa

Dm G Dm G [A DEFABB (Right hand) start] C Cmaj7 F C Cmaj7 F [CBGEA (x4) CBGEGA] Cmaj7 [BCDDEEE] F [CFEC] (x2) Cmaj7 F (x2) Bb (x2) Bb [CCDDCD] Eb [Bb D# D Bb] Ab Db Ab Db F#m Bm F#m Bm Amaj Emaj Amaj (Ab)

Schmetterling

Dm G Dm G [A DEFABB (Right hand) start] C Cmaj7 F C Cmaj7 F [CBGEA (x4) CBGEGA] Cmaj7 [BCDDEEE] F [CFEC] (x2) Cmaj7 F (x2) Bb (x2) Bb [CCDDCD] Eb [Bb D# D Bb] Ab Db Ab Db F#m Bm F#m Bm Amaj Emaj Amaj (Ab)

Butterfly

Dm G Dm G [A DEFABB (Right hand) start] C Cmaj7 F C Cmaj7 F [CBGEA (x4) CBGEGA] Cmaj7 [BCDDEEE] F [CFEC] (x2) Cmaj7 F (x2) Bb (x2) Bb [CCDDCD] Eb [Bb D# D Bb] Ab Db Ab Db F#m Bm F#m Bm Amaj Emaj Amaj (Ab)

Papillon

Dm G Dm G [A DEFABB (Right hand) start] C Cmaj7 F C Cmaj7 F [CBGEA (x4) CBGEGA] Cmaj7 [BCDDEEE] F [CFEC] (x2) Cmaj7 F (x2) Bb (x2) Bb [CCDDCD] Eb [Bb D# D Bb] Ab Db Ab Db F#m Bm F#m Bm Amaj Emaj Amaj (Ab)

Edytka Butterfly

D C Csus2 D C Csus2 D A Asus2 Em Amaj Asus2 (if finger not D) D C Csus2 D Em Amaj Asus2 (and pinkie on D) D C Csus2 D C Csus2 Em Amaj Asus2 (pinkie on D)

BLUE BOOK

Butterfly 2

Dm Gm Dm Gm Cmaj7 F Cmaj7 F Cmaj7 F Cmaj7 F Bb Eb Bb Eb Ab C# (Db) Ab D# (Eb) Ab D# Emaj Amaj Emaj Amaj Emaj Amaj Emaj Amaj

Butterfly 3

D Asus2 Am D Asus2 Am D Asus2 Am D Asus2 Am Chorus: Em A Asus2

Chardonnay 2

Verses: Dm G Dm G Cmaj7 F Cmaj7 F Dm G Dm G Cmaj7 F Cmaj7 F Chorus: Bm F#m D Am D Am Bm F#m Bm F#m D Am D Am

Cold Outside (your Love) Silver and Gold Version

Verse: G D# G D# A# G# A# G# Gm Chorus: Am A# F E Bm F#m G Em Bm A Em A Em G Bm G Bm Emaj

La Farfalla

D G D G [A DEFABB (Right hand) start] C F C F [CBGEA (x4) CBGEGA] C [BCDDEEE] F [CFEC] (x2)

C F (x2) Bb (x2) Bb [CCDDCD] Eb [Bb D# D Bb] Ab Db Ab Db F#m Bm F#m Bm Amaj Emaj Amaj (Ab)

La mia farfalla

G D Am Em A Em A Em G B G B G D Asus2 Em G D Asus2 Em Am Em A Em

Mariposa 2

Dm G Dm G [A DEFABB (Right hand) start] C C Cmaj7 F C Cmaj7 F [BCDDEEE CFEC (x2)] Cmaj7 F [BCDDEEE] F [CFEC] (x2)

Cmaj7 F (x2) Bb (x2) Bb [CCDDCD] Eb [Bb D# D Bb] Ab Db Ab Db Bb D F Bb Amaj Emaj Amaj (Ab)

Quizás (Spanish Translation of Maybe)

D D (No top E string) Chorus: Emaj G D

The Same Old Slow Dance

Verse: D Am D Am F C Bb G Chorus: C Bb Ab G (plus Bb)

Melody: D# D# C (+D#) D# D# C Ab Db Ab Db

Bridge + Instrumental Am Fm Em Fm Em Fm

Schmetterling (1)

Dm G Dm G [A DEFABB (Right hand) start] C Cmaj7 F C Cmaj7 F [CBGEA (x4) CBGEGA] Cmaj7 [BCDDEEE] F [CFEC] (x2)

Cmaj7 F (x2) Bb (x2) Bb [CCDDCD] Eb [Bb D# D Bb] Ab Db Ab Db F#m Bm F#m Bm Amaj Emaj Amaj (Ab)

Schmetterling (Ich vergesse dich nie)

Dm G Dm G [A DEFABB (Right hand) start] C Cmaj7 F C Cmaj7 F [CBGEA (x4) CBGEGA] Cmaj7 [BCDDEEE] F [CFEC] (x2)

Cmaj7 F (x2) Bb (x2) Bb [CCDDCD] Eb [Bb D# D Bb] Ab Db Ab Db F#m Bm F#m Bm Amaj Emaj Amaj (Ab)

[1] From 'Norfolk' by John Betjeman.

[2] Title of a song by ZZ Top

[3] Title of a film Town Without Pity (1961), directed by Gottfried Reinhardt. With Kirk Douglas, Barbara Rütting, Christine Kaufmann. Gene Pitney sings 'Town without Pity' to accompany the film and the song was later covered by Ronnie Montrose.

[4] Ironic play on the Beatles song 'Let it be'.

[5] La Vita è Bella (1997) is coincidentally the title of a film directed by Roberto Benigni, starring Roberto Benigni, Nicoletta Braschi and Giorgio Cantarini.

[6] Born Free (1966) is a film directed by James H. Hill and produced by Sam Jaffe and Paul Radin with a musical score by John Barry. It commences with a song sung by Matt Munro, and stars Virginia McKenna and Bill Travers

[7] The opening words to 'Vincent' sung by Don Mclean are 'Starry, Starry night.'

[8] 'That whatsoever King may reign, I will be the Vicar of Bray, Sir!' are verses from the poem entitled 'The Vicar of Bray' in The British Musical Miscellany, Volume I, 1734. Text as found in R. S. Crane, A Collection of English Poems 1660-1800. New York: Harper & Row, 1932.

[9] Singin' in the Rain (1952) directed by Stanley Donen and Gene Kelly. With Gene Kelly, Donald O'Connor, Debbie Reynolds

[10] My Fair Lady (1964), directed by George Cukor; with Audrey Hepburn, Rex Harrison, and Stanley Holloway.